I'M 50 AND NOT OUT

Life does not end at 50 it just keeps getting better.
My world is filled with mishaps and complete chaos.

Nancy George

I'm 50 and Not Out

Nancy George

This book is a work of non-fiction. All rights reserved. No part of this publication may be reproduced, distributed, or transmitted in any form or by any means, including photocopying, recording, or other electronic or mechanical methods, without the prior written permission of the publisher, except in the case of brief quotations embodied in critical reviews and certain other non-commercial uses permitted by copyright law. For permission requests, write to the author, information provided for your convenience "Connect with Me Online" at the end of the book.

ISBN-13: 9781790771059

Editing by Swish Design & Editing
Formatting by Swish Design & Editing
Cover design by Book Cover by Design
Cover Image Copyright 2018

DEDICATION

I dedicate this book to my husband who encouraged
me to put pen to paper and has been with me through
thick and thin.

To all women of the world, who like me have husbands,
children, pets and a home to juggle, and we do it with
no awards, recognition or payment.
I am the CEO of my home, the Chairman of the Board.

This is my life. It is filled with chaos – no day is ever
dull.

My motto…
Just keep calm
and have
another wine or chocolate.

BLURB

Life does not end at 50, it's just a new beginning. To all the women of the world, who like me have a husband, children, pets and a home to juggle, we do it with no awards, recognition or payment.

My life in words.

This is the story of one woman whose life is filled with chaos, animals, children and a husband, but it's also filled with laughter and tears.

From hot flushes, to a Brazilian wax job, to a G string, what could possibly go wrong?

I'M 50 AND NOT OUT

FORWARD

If it's hard at 50.

What the hell is going to happen

when I reach 60?

CHAPTER 1

It's my birthday...

"Happy 50th," screamed my girlfriend down the telephone. "Gosh, what's it like to be the big 50? It's all downhill from here... wrinkles, unwanted hair, and not to mention the wobbly bits. Ha-ha, when I get to 50, you'll be close to 60. Where's the party, or will you have to be in bed by seven, you poor old thing. Love you." And then she hung up.

Silently I stood by the phone thinking. I've just woken up as this old wrinkled hairy person, and how dare she talk about wobbly bits. What's going on, all I've done is go to bed as a 49-year-old young chick and woken up as a broken old hag. Who else knows about things that are personal to me?

I spoke too soon when the phone started to ring.

"Happy 50th, you old trout. You're on your way to 60, then 70, and then God knows… you'll be sitting in a corner dribbling in a home for the bewildered. Talk soon, must have a catch-up," yelled my cousin down the line and then she hung up.

God strike her dumb.
Banish her to a hole in a wall.
Shut up all of you.
This is too much for me.
I need to seek solace and go somewhere quiet.

As I shuffled up the hallway to my bathroom, I thought perhaps a nice hot bath would do the trick. Yes, 50-year-old people do that sort of thing, don't they? Now I'm on the way down this bloody hill heading for a black hole, to a place where 50-year-old post-menopausal ladies go. Holy cow! I've just had a terrible thought, *if it's this way at 50 what in God's name will happen to me when I reach 60?*

Stop the world I want to get off.

CHAPTER 2

Every 50-year-old woman has wobbly bits – well don't they?

Lately, I seem to be spending a lot of time in the bathroom. God, how I hate catching a look at myself when I come out of the shower. What happened to the taut, tight flat tummy, the perky breasts? I know they're in here somewhere, it's just a matter of finding them and getting them back in place. Instead, my tummy has a bulge a bit like a small mountain range. My breasts well, they need a helping hand sometimes, so a wonder bra is great news as my cleavage comes together rather nicely.

My weight seems to control my whole universe. Let's face it, the days of being a petite size 10 are well gone. That was a long time ago, lost to history, now I seem to move between a 14 and a 16, and if I get very ill, I can get to a size 12. Bloody hell, this being 50 is a pain in the neck.

Yesterday I didn't have any of these thoughts. Now I'm a complete wreck. Wait a minute, just when I think things could not get any worse now, I have facial hair? I'm sure that was not there yesterday.

To sum up my morning – I have wrinkles, I'm on the downward slide, my wobbly bits wobble, and now I have facial hair – kill me now and get it over with.

CHAPTER 3

Am I sexy – well, am I?

It's hard to say at this point, after all, I am standing in front of the bathroom mirror in my pajamas with a touch of mascara under my right eye. Hmmm… do I feel sexy? I'll ask my husband. No, better not he's in bed with his mouth wide open snoring.

What have I become?

What happened to this happy girl who loved nothing better than the feel of silk on her skin? Where has she gone? Look at me! My PJ's speak for themselves. They have teddy bears on them. What am I thinking?

I'm now suicidal as I pay close attention to my reflection in the mirror?

I need to focus!

Okay, I sometimes wear knickers that hold my tummy in, and I wear wooly vests with lace under my clothes, so that's what everybody does, don't they? But I look into my eyes ignoring the smudged mascara, the hair all over the place, the PJ's with bears and absolutely no makeup on and who do I see? I see a 50-year-old woman, who runs a home, who juggles kids and a husband, who cleans, cooks, feeds many cats, listens to everyone's gripes, who never gets the channel changer. I am a wife, mother, lover, and feeder of various pets, *so there!*

CHAPTER 4

The gentle art of seduction. In my case, there's nothing gentle about it!

Now picture this, we all have that moment when we decide to be sexy beasts – you know that night we plan to be a tigress in the bedroom. Why is it in my case it never seems to go according to plan. Either the kids ring wanting something now, or visitors seem to appear and don't want to go home, or my husband feels sick or is tired.

When we finally get to the bedroom, I picture in my mind that grand entrance when I emerge from the bathroom looking gorgeous. I'm usually confronted with my husband snoring.

But this time he's awake as I poke my head around the corner of the bathroom. Our eyes meet, I move slowly towards the bed, his arms are outstretched. There's just one more step to take and fuck it. I get my foot caught in my handbag strap. Mental note: *never to put purse by the bed.* I fall, extensive carpet burns on my knees, and now in a lot of pain.

Husband rolls about the bed laughing. Me? I get into bed still in pain and bleeding from the carpet burn on my knees. So the husband gives me a quick peck on the cheek. "Come on, old girl, lights out it's sleep time."

Another mental note: *no more sexy nights.*

CHAPTER 5

Dinner for two. A night out. Romance. This has disaster written all over it!

You know I think it's just easy to stay at home. Now picture this scene, the love of my life arrives home and announces, "Honey, tonight I'm taking you out, just me and you."

"What? Are you insane? What shall I wear? God my hair, my nails, how much time have I got?"

"Hurry up, we're leaving at 7:00pm sharp."

Oh, shit it's 6:00pm now. I race like a sprinter to the shower, wash all the significant bits, powder hangs in the air and settles on the floor and mirror. Good, I can't see myself. It's also on the ceiling, the blinds, too bloody bad I'll clean it up later.

Now, what to wear. Good question. I try on everything. Nah, hate this. God, this looks terrible. I announce, "I can't go, I have nothing to wear."

"Don't be silly, wear anything, you always look good to me."

Okay on that note, I put on the very first thing I tried on. Dressing room looking like a hurricane has just passed – will clean that up later.

Set off in husband's truck. The smell of freshly picked grass wafts in the air. I suddenly realize there's a hay bale in the back of the truck. No, it's worse, I am sitting in the grass. I have hay stuck to my bum, it's in my hair. My window won't close properly, it's cold, I can't feel my face. Husband's oblivious to my discomfort – I've married an idiot.

We finally arrive at the restaurant – our table is waiting. I have hay stuck to my boot, my hair, it's bloody everywhere, and people are staring. I remain calm. I act normal. Another mental note: *kill husband.* I can't wait for this evening to end.

Oh crap, our neighbors are here, and they're approaching.

Shelia – nicknamed motor mouth – starts talking, "What have you been up to"?

"Oh, nothing Shelia. We came in the truck, and it had a hay bale in it."

"Stop telling fibs," said my husband. "To tell the truth, the old girl was randy, and we had a snog in the car before we came in. You know, when you're in the mood, you just have to go for it."

I want to die now. I wish the floor would open and drag me through.

My husband talks rather loudly, everyone heard and I am now a lush.

Oh my God, this man's looking strangely at me. Oh shit, he's just winked. He thinks I'm easy.

Must find on the internet the penalty for the murder of a husband!.

CHAPTER 6

Is that new? What this old thing?

Why is it we sneak clothes in? Sometimes I get caught out because I leave the label on. Other times my husband will say, "Is that new?"

My comment is usually, "This old thing? Don't you remember I wore this when we went to your mother's for dinner? You made the comment that you liked it."

"Oh, did I?"

What a sucker. Husbands have no idea. For instance, in both bathrooms, I have wooden blinds on the windows. He's oblivious to this. I get my hair cut and colored, and it's weeks before he notices, and then he says, "Christ, what have you done to your hair?" But he's very quick to point out, "Has your bum got bigger?" Who put him in charge of bums? Is my husband the bum police? There's nothing wrong with my bum provided I don't look at it.

On close inspection of my wardrobe, I have to admit I've made some fashion mistakes. For example, the size 10 dress although in basic black and very smart, what was I thinking? I can't get into a size 10.

I will paint you a picture. Me standing in front of my mirror yet again. Taking the dress off the hanger, slipping dress onto the wobbly body. It's gets stuck on my breasts. Wait a minute to catch my breath then wriggle a bit more gently, sliding it down over hips. Tummy's sticking out, I look 6 months pregnant. Hmmm… I look like big Bertha who was in my class at school. I bet today she is a petite size

8. I hate myself. What was I ever thinking that one day I could wear this? Dumb, dumb, dumb, pathetic Nancy, will you never learn. And the terrible part is I keep on doing it, and I'm sure I'm stupid.

Now, I'm having trouble getting this thing off. So, after struggling, I put it back on the hanger in dark depths of wardrobe never to see the light of day but now feeling very depressed. I just can't win, being 50 is quite crappy.

CHAPTER 7

Housework, who invented this word?

I'm sure I am not the only woman in the world who seems to get sidetracked when doing housework. Because I work, it's usually done on a Saturday morning.

Now, picture this. I start with our bed. I begin by changing the sheets, then move to the laundry and put the sheets in the washing machine. I go back to the bedroom, then remember to go to linen cupboard to get new sheets. On the way see a mark on the carpet, so I go to the kitchen to get the cleaner. See that the kitchen is in a mess, so I begin to tidy the kitchen. Notice rubbish bin needs to be emptied. Go outside through laundry, put trash down as washing machine has washed sheets and proceed to wash line to hang up sheets. Remember that the towels in the bathroom need to be removed along with the clothes. Walk past rubbish, linen cupboard, and unmade bed to get towels and clothes. Remark to myself I must get clean sheets for the bed, nearly trip over garbage, put towels on to wash. Take rubbish to the bin. Notice garden has a few weeds, start weeding. Remember bed needs sheets, go back inside. The cat starts to meow, so I pick it up and give it a cuddle, take it to the kitchen, feed cat. Notice carpet cleaner on the bench, and remember the stain on the carpet. Remove the stain, proceed to linen cupboard to get sheets, go into the bedroom, put sheets on the bed and begin to make the bed. See dressing table needs a dusting. Leave bed and proceed once more to the kitchen to get a duster. Go back to bedroom see that the bed's half unmade, finish bed.

Decide I need a coffee. Sit down for 10 minutes totally exhausted. Continue through rest of day getting nowhere when finally I'm ready for bed, and I see the duster sitting on dressing the table!

CHAPTER 8

Husbands… hmmm?

What is it about men? I once heard that God made men late Sunday afternoon and women first thing Monday morning.

Take my husband for instance. When it comes to cleaning up the kitchen, he seems to think that water and lots of it are how you do it, and the bench is covered from one end to the other with water. He will put a large dinner plate with two baked potatoes in the fridge – it would not occur to him to get a smaller plate. He has been known to leave empty plates in the refrigerator. He insists on doing the washing which is great. He's just has not grasped that laundry should be separated because everything goes into the washing machine together and my white underwear sometimes has been changed to a lovely shade of pink mainly because he washed it with his red T-shirt. But wait, it gets worse. He lovingly hangs the washing on the clothesline. Sometimes he puts 3 pegs to hang one pair of knickers, and the tablecloth, towels, and sheets are never even on the line. Still, the washing gets dry, and it's one job I don't have to do.

What about the channel changer? When I'm watching a movie, he suddenly flicks it to something else, it drives me crazy. I'm sure it's part of his anatomical makeup, and I only get it if he's asleep or away. He has his chair and his little table which always has an empty cup, plus the endless papers which just lie there until I pick them up. He attempts to make the bed – God forbid if my mother were alive, she would be mortified – but he has no idea that the bedspread should be straight and the pillows should be placed not thrown from a distance.

I once made his favorite carrot cake. On feeling a bit peckish, I decided a nice cup of coffee and cake was the answer. When I lifted the lid on the cake tin, I was greeted with cake, knife and no frosting, he'd eaten the lot. Or worse still, he leaves the top off the biscuit tin, and everything goes soft.

When we're in bed, he suddenly breaks wind. He has this nasty habit of throwing the sheet over my face – I can't breathe, and man does he smell. He thinks it's funny. He starts to laugh. What a pea size brain he has.

I *will* get my revenge, and all I can say at this point is, *be afraid, be bloody afraid.*

CHAPTER 9

Children – are like joyous angels.

Whoever said that is a complete idiot! Oh flip, I just did. What was I thinking?

They are a constant hunger machine. I have two boys – food, sleep, and dirty washing seem to be a number one priority in their life. Don't get me wrong, I adore my kids. It's just, I always seem to be at the grocery shop or beside the washing machine.

Day after day they emerge from their caves, walking around in a sleepy daze opening the fridge, full inspection, close the fridge and then announce,

"Why don't we have any food?" The fridge is stocked with fruit and vegetables, but to them, we have no food. However, if the refrigerator were stocked with McDonald's, K.F.C. and Burger King, they would be in heaven.

It was me who gave them the big sex talk, or at least I thought. They both let me go red in the face, shuffle around the conversation and then they had the cheek to get up kiss me on the top of my head and say, "We learned all that at school. Been there done that." On confronting my husband with my embarrassing moment, all he said was, "My boys are okay. They know about girls," and off he walked whistling leaving me all alone to contemplate my embarrassment.

Why me? Why do I have to take all this crap? Because I love them and they love me, and I would never change one thing.

Forget that I complain, I love them all – sometimes.

I wonder if this makes me a bad mother?

CHAPTER 10

Girlfriends – are like old songs, their melody never stops.

Never mind the fact that I think my friends should be struck dumb for wishing me their kind of happy birthday.

My girlfriend, Susan, is the only person in the world who listens to my fears, my dreams, my new diet plans as well as my old ones. She is the lady who shared my secret about being so in love with this boy that went to my school. She was the one who rang him up and told him that I was keen on him. She took me to the pictures, and we all sat in the back row. She was there when I had my first kiss – she is my best friend. The only thing wrong with this picture is that I can't remember my great love. *What the hell was his name?*

And then I have Amanda, a very true friend, Allison, Val, Jo and Theresa. I adore them all.

Girlfriends are amazing, treasure them. There are times I wish they would vanish from the face of the earth however, especially when they telephone me right in the middle of my favorite program. But then again they always seem to contact me when I need to talk to a friend. They are darlings, and I love them.

I'm also blessed to have three sisters-in-law, I love them, and I'm fortunate to have these beautiful ladies in my life.

CHAPTER 11

Every home should have a pet. I have 8!
Perhaps my brain is clouded with candy floss.

I know what you're all thinking, what is it with this woman. Well, you see, they sort of pick me, and I am a soft touch when it comes to animals. God forbid if I ever got a job at the SPCA! Nope, I just donate food instead.

Now, let me introduce my babies. We have Custard, Toby, Poppy, Tiger, Charlie and Mac (all cats) and then Leo a 12-year-old Jack Russell and Suzy my Labrador puppy. Our house is filled with chaos mainly due to me, but you know I wouldn't change one thing. Most days are spent stepping over cats as they lie on the heated tiles, or making the bed around Poppy, or putting off the ironing as Custard has found a soft spot on my husband's bush shirts, or not picking up the paper as Mac is asleep on it. Most nights I'm up and down letting cats in, letting cats out. Poppy is allowed to sleep with me. Usually, it's just the three of us in bed, but on cold, rainy, thundery nights there are six of us all snuggled up.

I absolutely hate them when they bring to my door their latest kill which ranges from birds, mice, rats, and the occasional ferret. That's when I have to play funeral director and dispense with the dead – which is always cremation. That's the big negative about having animals.

When I see one sitting outside the door looking cold and miserable, muggins here, gets up to let them in. They look at me and just meow. Then they begin to clean themselves while I stand to attention obediently waiting for a pussycat to come inside. I wonder why we let cats rule our lives? That's because dogs have owners, but cats have staff.

Leo has a severe wind problem which smells disgusting, and Suzy loves to carry things in her mouth.

I don't know why I really wrote this chapter, I guess it's for no other reason than to tell you I love animals.

I remember when my mother passed away, I went to lie down as I needed a quiet place. All my babies came with me, they knew I was in pain, and they repeated this gesture of love when my dad died. They felt my pain, and somewhere between my tears, Poppy and Toby licked my face and snuggled close to me, giving me their love. They are a comfort, and I adore them.

CHAPTER 12

Nana – bugger…

"Mum, guess what? We're going to have a baby. Look, I can't talk right now but will phone you tomorrow. Goodbye Granny! Don't forget to tell Dad."

For goodness sake what's going on in my world? I'm 50. I have wrinkles. And now, I'm going to be a nana! This is too much. I'm far too young.

I remember my nana, she was in her 70's and wore pearls, lace, and twin sets. Nana, like bloody hell I am, this grandchild can call me Nancy. Right, that's sorted. What rubbish is it to be called Granny or Nana. Nope, it's going to be Nancy.

Nine months later we got the call. "It's a boy. 8 pounds 1, and man has he got hair."

Baxter came into my life on the 21st September 2010, and as I look at him sleeping, I wonder what he will do with his life. Will he be a future Prime Minister, rugby player, doctor, painter, poet or writer...?

CHAPTER 13

Nana – again! Bugger, bugger...

Our youngest telephoned one evening. "Guess what? We're pregnant."

Oh my God, another baby? I've just gotten used to the first one, now another.

There was no time to dwell on this fact as Charlotte arrived on the 16th February 2011. Our little princess is so special. I wish her God's blessing, peace on earth and may her world be filled with happiness and love. May all her dreams be answered? And I pray to God above that she does not turn out to be a diva from hell and I have to babysit her.

CHAPTER 14

And again! Bugger me.

Another telephone call to announce another baby and a brother for Baxter. Reid arrived on the 15th January 2014. I love him. He fears nothing, he loves his food, and he is content.

I wish for him to have all his dreams come true, and to be the best in whatever field he chooses.

One more time the phone went. "Guess what? It's baby number two. A sister for Charlotte."

Darling Elizabeth was born on the 6th of March. I wish for her peace, love, and hope, to be the best she can be.

After all this, my darlings can call me whatever they like. I don't care. I love them, and I love being a nana.

Thank you, God.

CHAPTER 15

Hair removal – ooouuuccchhh!

My girlfriend, who has been removed from my Christmas card list for the third time, decided to treat us both to getting our legs waxed.

"Susan," I said, "Will it hurt? You know my pain threshold is about zero."

"Don't be silly, of course, it won't. It's just like taking a sticky plaster off. That only stings for a tiny bit."

"Well, if you're sure." I start to get excited and I can't wait. Just think, in an hour I will have silky smooth legs. Yay, no more using a razor.

At exactly 1:30pm we arrived at the Monique Beauty House. "Good afternoon, ladies," said the rather petite receptionist. "Please take a seat. Mrs. Susan you will see Gail, and Mrs. Nancy you will see Monique. She does the Brazilian," she said with this smirk on her face.

I whispered to Susan, "Why is she looking at me? What is a Brazilian?"

"It's nothing," said Susan. "It's just a name for hair removal."

"Okay, what are you having?"

"I have a full leg?"

Suddenly the door opened, and there in her glory was Monique, a vibrant lady with bright red lipstick, dark black hair, and she's utterly gorgeous.

"Hello, Mrs. Nancy, please come this way. Have you ever had your legs waxed before?"

"No," I replied. "Never."

"I must say you're very adventurous asking for a Brazilian. You understand what's involved?

"Yes, it's just getting rid of hair, isn't it?"

"Quite, my dear. Please hop up on the table, and we will begin."

Slowly she started putting warm wax on my calf and then she gently applied a cloth. "Now this will only smart for a few seconds."

Rip went the fabric. *Shit,* I thought, *that bloody well hurt.*

"Well done. Let's continue."

My pain register was in overdrive – please God let this be finished.

After agonizing pain, Monique finally said, "Okay, I've finished your legs. They look fantastic, so soft."

I had to admit that pain aside, my legs felt wonderful.

"Now, my dear, it's time for the Brazilian. Please remove your underwear."

"*What?* Remove my underwear? Monique, I don't understand."

"Relax, here let me help you. Oh my God, did I put good knickers on? Please God let the answer to that question be yes. I will go to church every Sunday. I will say prayers every day. I looked down and to my embarrassment I had my red knickers that my darling husband has washed in bleach, and they were a sort of pink and white. I hate myself. Mental note: *Never wear shitty underwear.*

Okay, now spread your left leg. *Help Me.* My privates are exposed to this cow with the red lips. Oh hell, she's put hot wax on my pubic hairs. *What the hell is she doing?*

"Now dear, on my word I want you to breathe in, and when I say please breathe out. Here we go. Good girl, take a big breath in, hold it, now breathe out."

Ooouuuccchhh! The pain. The pain. Yep, I'm going to faint. The pain. The suffering. Stop the bloody plain.

"Good girl. Now that side's done. Please spread your right leg, and we will do the other side."

There are not enough expletives to explain how I'm feeling right now.

"Now, my dear," said skank face, Monique. "All done. I hope madam is happy. I will get a mirror."

Swallow me up God, my privates are on show for the entire world to see.

"You look lovely. Please put your underwear on and get dressed. My receptionist will see to you."

As I walked into reception, Susan had this smirk and so did Miss Pointy-Ugly-Face. Yep, right there and then I wanted to smash her face. Susan told me that everyone in the waiting room heard me yell. I hate Susan. She's a bitch. How dare she cause me this pain?

I entered this so-called beauty shop as a well-mannered lady. I'm leaving with the thought of a serial killer.

"Oh Susan, how embarrassing. She saw all of my private things."

"Bloody hell, will you get over yourself. Everyone has a Brazilian. I do. I just didn't need one today. Now shut up and let's have a drink."

After I had got home, my husband shouted out, "How was your waxing?"

"Terrible," I told him. "They took it all," I whispered to him. "I have no hair on my body, not even on my privates."

Suddenly, he looked at me and said, "How about we go and play doctors and nurses?"

"Look here, you sex maniac, don't you understand? A strange woman looked at my bits. I'm so embarrassed. It's Susan's fault, she made the appointment. Everyone will hear about this. The shame, the shame," I cried.

"Come here," my husband said. "I'll give you a cuddle. No one will know. I won't tell. Now, how about my suggestion of doctors and nurses…"

"You are sex mad, do you know that?"

CHAPTER 16

Guess who's coming to dinner?

My husband announced one Friday morning that Bernard & Annabel, who had a surname I couldn't pronounce, were coming to dinner on Saturday. "Nothing special, darling, just something simple. And just because one is a doctor and the other a detective, remember they are ordinary people."

"Thank you, I will remember that."

Bernard was an ear nose and throat specialist and was lovely. He liked to spend time in the garden with his roses. But Annabel was a different kettle of fish, she was scary. Annabel was a police detective, and I would hate to get on the wrong side of her.

Of all the people in the world we had to invite them over for dinner. Right! Now, don't panic. I have recipe books. Okay, Joe Segar – let's do dinner easy-peasy style. After several reads of my recipes I decided to go with a chunky vegetable soup, a hearty beef casserole, followed by a fresh fruit salad, and to end, a selection of cheese and crackers.

The day of the great dinner party arrived. The house was clean, everything was perfect. I started on the vegetable soup – that was a breeze. The fresh fruit salad – easy-peasy. Now for the hearty beef casserole. Things started okay, it was a recipe I'd made before, one of my tried and true. I had it on the bench, turned around for a split second and when I turned back, Poppy my treasured cat, was walking along the bench towards my casserole.

What happened next was played out in slow motion. She walked up to it, put one paw into my yummy dish and hooked out a piece of steak, looked at me and went on her way. I swear to you this had never happened before.

What to do? Okay don't panic, it was only one little paw.

Oh my, God, I'm fucked! What if they have a reaction. As a doctor, he'll guess it's the food, and bloody Annabel will arrest me. Everyone will know I tried to commit murder by hearty beef casserole.

Bugger Poppy. As I looked out the window, I saw her, the scumbag little bitch, digging a hole in my garden with both paws. God, what the hell is in my dish! All sorts of stuff. I can't throw it away. I only have tins of baked beans, cheese on toast, and large roasts in the freezer which it was too late to thaw and cook. I won't tell anyone, it will be and Poppy's and my secret.

Promptly at 6:30pm they arrived. Bernard was charming, and to be fair so was Annabel. I guess when she's off duty she changes personality. The chunky veggie soup went down well. Now for my hearty beef. I was lost in conversation as we all finished loading our plates.

Now was the moment! Bernard put the casserole into his mouth, and he made the comment, "This is fantastic. Annabel hurry up and taste it. There's a flavor I can't quite put my finger on, perhaps it's a secret family recipe."

"Yes, Bernard, it is." I will take this secret to my grave. God if they only knew! What could I say? Perhaps something along the lines of... well, see that cat lying in front of the fire? The strange taste is poppy's left paw. The one she puts it in her mouth when she cleans her nails, and the one she walks on through dirt, grass, and the compost. That's my secret right there.

Thank God the evening finished at around 11:00pm. And as I prepared for bed, my husband finally said, "What a great night. Your meal was fantastic. Hey, what did you put in the casserole?"

"Nothing special," I replied. "Just Poppy's paw."

"You're joking, right?" he asked.

"Darling, would I tell you a fib? Course it's a joke. Imagine if the cat had put her paw in it? God forbid, it would be terrible. I can't imagine what would happen. Good night, God bless."

CHAPTER 17

Just what we don't need is another bloody cat!

Lucy came into our world a year ago and left us so suddenly. She was accidentally killed. She ruled our world, and we loved her for it. She was deaf, and she wore a collar with a bell, so we knew where she was at all times.

I just needed to tell you that I loved her so much and she loved me. There's a place in my heart that's broken, and I miss her every day. I wish I could have her back. Death is so cruel and unforgiving.

I love you Lucy, sweet dreams.

CHAPTER 18

Hot flushes – a punishment from hell!

My mother never told me about hot flushes. I remember waking up one winter's night covered in a cold, clammy sweat. I nudged my husband and said, "I think I'm ill."

"What's the matter," he mumbled?

"I've got something wrong with me. It's like I'm hot, and my jammies are all wet."

"Are you dead?" he said.

"No, I'm not dead."

"Then roll over and go to sleep."

"Roll over and go to sleep? I can't. There's something wrong with me."

After I'd taken a shower and put on fresh night clothes, I finally got to sleep at about 4:30am. This is not nice.

I telephoned Susan for advice. "Look…" she said, "… you're going through the change. That was a hot flush. Face it, you're at that age when your body is moving to the next level."

"Pray in the name of God… what is the next level? Senior citizenship. Old folks' home. Now listen here… I have a Brazilian, I wear cute underwear, let's not talk about bloody hot flushes."

"I tell you when you least expect it they sort of creep up. Bloody nasty beggars."

We were out at friends sitting around their fire, drinking mulled wine. Amanda's a lovely hostess, the food was glorious, the company perfect. I was at peace with the world. My karma was humming slowly when all of a sudden I felt the prickly sensation of my skin burning. *Oh no,* I thought, *here it comes.* My merino top stuck to me, I had water running between my breasts, so I needed to make a quick exit. In a hurry, I stepped over to the bathroom. Off went the top, cold water was splashed between my breasts, and I sat on Amanda's tiled floor to cool down. Thank God it only lasted a brief moment.

While sitting on the floor I had a talk with God, I put it to him... *why did you do this?* We women have to go through the pain of childbirth, looking after husbands and children, and then you go and do this to us?

I'm still waiting for his answer. Typical male, I've got the silent treatment.

CHAPTER 19

The G-string – whoever invented them should be tied up and left out in the rain.

My darling girlfriend Susan, who I should really consider ignoring for the rest of my life, what with the waxing and now with my new G-string. Why did I put her in charge of telling me which underwear I should buy?

It so happened we were going to dinner at our local club, so I thought I'd wear them. They really are a lovely pale pink with lace – very sexy. We set off, and I felt beautiful and a little naughty. I kept winking at my husband who asked, "What's wrong with your eye? You keep squinting. Sort yourself out before we arrive at the club."

"I will," I replied. "It must be dust." I was sort of wriggling on my seat.

"What the hell is wrong with you, have you got fleas?"

"Oh, it's nothing," I lied. Actually, I was a bit uncomfortable. My inside butt cheeks were screaming with pain. Obviously, the G-string was a little tight, and the pain was so bad I felt sick. The whole thing had ridden and stuck to places where things should not get stuck.

Ouch! I couldn't walk. Every step I took brought tears to my eyes.

My husband and I were talking to our friends, Theresa and Trevor, who were looking at me strangely and asking me if I was all right. I told them I had sore eyes due to dust. Trevor replied with a,

"No worries. I believe they're playing our song. Shall we?"

For fuck's sake, I want out! I don't want to dance around the floor with this idiot, and if he twirls me one more time, I will swing him a blow from hell. I have a severe case of chaffing right now. How will I ever be able to look my doctor in the face, or even talk to my chemist about this? Thank God the bloody music stopped. "Do you want another dance, Nan?"

"No, no. I need to go to the ladies room. I'll sit these dances out." I ran to the bathroom, and there in the privacy of my cubicle, I took my G-string off. The relief was indescribable. Now, where do I put it? Only one place – my bra. Perfect! As good a hiding place as any.

Walking back to the table was pure magic. My darling husband said, "Come on, old girl, this waltz in ours." It truly was magic us dancing cheek to cheek, how romantic. As the music faded, another one started, Rock around the Clock. "Okay, let's show these young ones how to actually dance." It was unbelievable. We rocked, we rolled, and we did everything. Thank God I was wearing trousers. My husband whispered to me, "Don't look but someone has lost their knickers, it might be one of those four women with dresses on."

"What are you talking about?" Look over there, glance at the floor, and yep someone had lost their knickers. I just don't believe it. I gently felt my left breast, and you guessed it, my knickers lay there on the floor for everyone to see. And to make matters worse, our MC made a joke of it over the loudspeakers. Some lady picked them up and threw them in the rubbish bin.

Come on, give me a break, I had made a solemn pledge to the good Lord above, and I hoped he heard me that this was my first and only time I shall ever wear a G-string.

The next day I telephoned Susan, and all she could do was laugh for about 10 minutes. "Don't worry, next time just purchase a bigger size."

"Listen here... there won't be a next time." As I hung up the telephone, she was still laughing.

CHAPTER 20

Memories – are locked away in my heart.

Memories are beautiful. Some are sad, and some are filled with such joy.

The sudden passing of my dear friend to cancer. My beloved parents, my aunty and my in-laws
When I think about them, I brings a tear to my eyes.

The happy ones make life worth it. My husband, my children, grandchildren, daughters-in-law, friends, roses, Fantails, cats, dogs, newborn lambs, baby calves, cherry trees, and brilliant sunsets.

I adore life, and although it's filled with chaos would I change anything? Absolutely *not!* This is my lot, and I love it. I cannot believe I just said that.

CHAPTER 21

I'm on a diet – yet again.

I am sick, sick, sick of putting on weight. Okay, I have to admit I have a sweet tooth. And yes, I have a fondness for chocolate, Pavlovas, cupcakes, peanut slabs, and chocolate bars. But on the other hand, I do go for walks. I eat wholemeal bread and limit my alcohol to one or two glasses of wine, and with all this, I still put on weight. I know I said earlier about bits that wobble, it's just that lately everything is wobbling. But on a good note, my boobs have gotten bigger. Someone told me they are fat deposits – all I can say is bring it on fat.

I have a Weight Watchers book, and I do try. Honestly, I do. It's just every time I go into a shop for a coffee I give way to temptation, and I end up eating the chocolate nibbles. I can't help it they look so delicious they're screaming to me 'eat me, eat me' and then when I've finished I always feel guilty.

But seriously I'm dieting, and hopefully, when you get to the end of this fantastic story, I will be back to my beloved size 12. I don't live in the real world that will *not* happen.

CHAPTER 22

Family – a time of forgiveness and love.

Once you get through the chaos of Christmas, it is lovely. It's the one time when our family can sit together, talk, laugh, play silly games, drink, eat and enjoy each other. Gone and forgotten are the angry words, the forgotten to say thank you. We are at peace. The old year is coming to an end. When I am at Mass, I pray for those people who have gone before me. I look at the stars and imagine they're shining down on me, filling me with love and peace. As the New Year approaches, I look forward to stepping into a brand-new squeaky-clean year, where I pray for no more violence, child abuse, murders, rapes, home invasions, and drunk drivers. But alas, I know we don't live in a perfect world.

CHAPTER 23

Supermarkets – one word #$%@

I can't for the life of me remember who put me in charge of going to the supermarket and I hate it because every time I stuff it up. I go in with a list, and do I stick to my list? No, no, no. I don't know why I bother. I have a budget of what I needed to spend, do I stick to my budget. No, no, no. I go in to buy two things, bread and milk, do I stick to these two things. No, no, no. Why, why, why can't I stick to it. I have no doubt a lot of other women go off the rails with their lists too. We can't help it.

I'm 50 and Not Out

I see a brightly colored bottle of shampoo, or coffee, or a new chocolate wrap and I think, *ooh that looks nice.* I guess a lot of women like me buy with our eyes.

I hate it when my husband decides to accompany me to the supermarket. He spends all day looking and reading the labels. Why? I don't care about the fat content, I just want to get my shopping over and done with.

Another thing I dislike is operators and packaging people who insist on talking about what they did that night. And how she met a guy named Nick. He was hot! Well, listen up Nick, I don't give a fat rats arse how hot you are, I just want to get out of this place. The quicker this love forlorn girl packs my groceries, the better. After all, I could be standing here stark naked, and she would not know.

Again, I hate shopping. And will I be going back next week? Yes, yes, yes and will I stick to my list? No, no, no. And will I have the same complaint? Yes, yes, yes.

CHAPTER 24

Wash day – it's not what it seems!

Every now and again I decide to wash the dog. I get the doggy shampoo and the tub, filling it up with warm water, put some flea mixture in it, after that I'm ready. But where is that little scumbag, Leo? You know I'm sure he deliberately disappears on me.

I spend minutes trying to find this walking flee factory. The worse thing is no one will help me. Usually, I don't have a long search, as he likes to hide under the bed or behind the woodpile. I keep telling him that he's about to have a warm, bubble bath but will he listen to me? No way.

The sad thing about this picture is that I always get wet from head to toe. You would think I'd remember Leo's little ploy of standing graciously still while I bath him, and then when I least expect it, he shakes himself and the excess water always lands on me. I have to admit though, that he always ends up smelling sweet for at least half an hour.

This is a dangerous job bathing a dog, but someone has to do it.

Nancy George

CHAPTER 25

My parents – thank you for just being there.

I was blessed with wonderful parents. My mother was a lady, she was tidy and a good homebody. I remember the homemade biscuit tins would always be filled. Our home was always clean. She had a love for everyone, and everyone adored her.

My father was a dreamer. He dreamed about winning the lotto. He could tell stories that were magical. We had an extraordinary story about a racehorse called "Lord Thingamabob." He won every race in the world, and I was his owner. I loved that story, and I wish I could hear it one more time.

Perhaps when I get to heaven, Dad will tell it to me once more.

They were involved in a violent home invasion. I pray to God that I never have to go through anything like that again. To this day I still have to be counseled. When you see them with a face so badly bruised and cut, and you hear the word rape, that's the moment time stands still. You can't comprehend the scene of carnage. Yet, my mother who, before this incident had survived major heart surgery came through like a trooper. We never mentioned it. My father, on the other hand, did not fare as well, because he could not protect my mother. He became a loner, his once laughing eyes grew dull and dead.

I sat with my mom the day she passed away. I held her hand and watched this incredible woman take her last breath. She brought me into this world, and I escorted her out. My darling Dad passed away in a rest home four years later in Auckland, with my brother holding his hand.

I never got to say goodbye to him. I love you, Dad. Take care, look after Mum and I will see you both again one day. xxxxxxxxx

CHAPTER 26

A visit to the vet – chaos runs riot!

There comes a time in everyone's life that you have to make a visit to the vet. Suzy, our lab, was looking a bit off-color. She wouldn't eat and for a Lab that's definitely a sign that she's sick. Muggins here was given the job of making the appointment and taking her on her first ever trip.

The easy part was the meeting time, the hardest was the questions. "Have her bowels moved and is her stool hard or mushy?"

Okay, like I follow my puppy around waiting for her to do her business. "I don't know," I told the person on the other end of the line.

"Hmmm, well bring her in. One must be more observant when one has a puppy," she said. I tried, but in a nice way, to tell her that one does not follow one's puppy around watching one's puppy's bottom in case one's puppy has a crap.

Our appointment time was for 2:00pm. Suzy was so eager to get into the car. *This will be a breeze,* I thought. Mental note: *never ever think that again*.

We pulled up at the Benmore Vet Hospital. *There must be money in pets,* I thought. This building was an old, rather beautiful two-story villa, with roses growing over the large entranceway, and the scent was absolutely amazing. Two large double doors opened, and Suzy refused to move, she would not take one step, fear had overcome her, so she lay flat with all four paws outstretched. The doors continued to open and shut on her.

"Move Suzy," I hissed.

"Are you having trouble with your dog?" yelled the receptionist rather loudly.

"No, she's just a bit scared. Give me a moment, please."

"For the love of God, Suzy, move your bloody backside. People have to step over you."

"Well, she will have to come in. The vet will certainly not treat her on the doorstep."

Time for action, this woman is going to take charge. I grabbed her by the collar and dragged her in. She sort of slid from side to side, and the receptionist started to laugh. *The bitch,* I thought, *this is so embarrassing.*

"Well, look at it this way," I said rather loudly. "At least she is wiping the dust off your dirty floors."

Oh yes, Miss Perfect did not like that! But score one for me. I made it to the seat and prayed like hell Suzy would move when I needed her to.

The door opened, and out stepped the most fantastic Mr. Hunk of the entire universe. "Suzy, hello girl, what's the matter with you?" And right on cue she sat bolt upright, and walked unaided into the consulting room. I kid you not, what a bitch. Mr. Hunk was so gentle with the scumbag. God, I want to come back as a small fluffy kitten. Mr. Fantastic can examine me, all over. *Ooohhh that would just be beautiful.*

Anyway back to reality. It seems Suzy's all ready to go. She just needed some worm tablets, and to keep an eye on her over the next couple of days. If there was no change, I was to bring her back. "I see you have another dog, Leo. He will need to be wormed also. When was the last time he came to the vet?"

"Oh, ages ago. I really don't remember. Well, I have a spare appointment at 3:00pm. Can you bring him in?"

I'm 50 and Not Out

"Yes, of course. I'll see you in half an hour."

I informed Miss Pointy-Nose that I would be back in 30 minutes with Leo. Now, let me tell you about Leo. He can be unpredictable sometimes. He's a gentle little man, and at other times he's a dog from the very depths of hell. On this occasion, he was the latter. The dog from hell arose from within his tiny body in an instant. Let me paint you a picture. Firstly, he started barking from the moment we entered the vet, and he never let up.

"Seems it's not your day," said Miss Perky-Face.

She was right, he just kept on barking. Then this rather large lady insisted on getting her cat out of the basket and onto her lap. Not a good idea when Leo's around. Apart from my cats at home, Leo hates all other cats. The chase was on, the lead slipped out of my hand. The cat jumped to the top of the bulk dog biscuits. Leo jumped halfway up, the cat howled, screamed and hissed. The large women was yelling. I was yelling. Miss Perky Face was screaming. Then the hunky vet came out and shouted, "Would everyone please be quiet."

Leo stopped. The cat stopped. The women stopped. I stopped. Miss perky face stopped.

I was ordered to the car where an examination took place on the dog from hell. Mental note: *must change vets.*

Told husband, he's still laughing. Another mental note: *have him committed to any sort of institute that will take him.*

CHAPTER 27

Holidays – so much trouble!

Have you ever had a day when the love of your life comes in and announces, "I think it's time for you and me to have a holiday? How do seven days in Rarotonga sound?"

"That sounds so lovely. I can't wait to just relax on the beach under a palm tree with nothing to do all day."

"Good. I knew you'd like that. Okay, you make all the arrangements," and with that, he walked back outside.

I knew this was too good to be true. Damn it, nothing's easy. If muggins here wanted a holiday, then muggins would have to book, plan and arrange. The thing is he had no idea what was involved, he just thought it's get tickets, book hotel, pack, arrive.

Firstly, I needed someone to feed the multitude of fur. Suzy and Leo would have to go to the dog kennels.

So, I started my list.
*Book kennels. Seven days in April. – Check.
*Get Jimmy next door to feed the cats. – Check.
*Book hotel. Somewhere on the beach with a beachfront room. 6-star resort. Beachside unit. – Check. If I have to do everything, then I want a great room and bugger the expense.

So, I telephoned our travel agent, and when I say our travel agent, it was Sally, and this was the first time I'd spoken to her – it sounds as if we do this all the time. Two adults, return from Auckland to

Rarotonga, and then she said the magic words, "For $200.00 more you could upgrade to business class, return."

*Flights booked, two adults Auckland to Rarotonga, business class. – Check.

Next, the most important thing which could make or break a holiday, the passports. That's easy, they're always kept in the office on the first shelf in a sealed bag. Mine is there, but where is 'he who thinks he should be obeyed?'

"Darling," I yell. "Have you seen your passport?"

"No," he yells back.

"It's not in the bag. When was the last time you saw it?"

"Don't know."

"Have you touched it?"

"Nope."

"Will you bloody well come here and think... no passport, no holiday. You must have moved it?"

"Nope."

"If you say nope one more time, I swear to God I will go on vacation by myself. Now bloody well think... did you take it out of the bag?"

"I can't remember."

"Shit! You only ever take the passport out of the bloody bag if we're going on holiday overseas."

Nothing's ever easy in this house. Suddenly, I knew that when one turns 50 all hell breaks loose and chaos abounds. I used to be in control of everything, now it's just slipping through my hands and I'm powerless to do anything about it.

"Look it has to be here somewhere. It did not get up, undo the plastic bag and go on a bloody holiday all by itself," I scream.

"Why are you crying?" my husband very quietly asks me.

"We were going to fly business class. We had a beachside unit," I cry. "Now it's all ruined 'cause of that scumbag passport."

"Oh dear," he says to me. "Do you mean this little black book which has my name on it? It must have slipped out onto the floor when you were opening it. Business class you say? Beachside unit you say? Well, you had better start packing." God, I hate him, especially when he has the upper hand.

I had another talk with God, and told him being 50 is crap. Everything had started to go wrong, and I asked him why, and like before I'm still waiting for his reply.

CHAPTER 28

Funerals – it's the end of the road!

I'm starting to get a tad worried. All my lovely aunts and uncles are starting to pop their clogs, which means somewhere down the road, I'm next, and I don't like it. To make matters worse, the other day I was in town looking at a building site wondering what sort of shop would fill the void when I noticed beside me a lovely gentleman, who like me, was wondering the same thing.

We stood for a while and chatted about things, our town, children, marriage. Then he introduced himself, "I'm Archie Forester. You may have heard of us, we are the local funeral directors."

Crap! When I die, this lovely man will see my tatty bits. Death is all around me, I've become a professional funeral mourner.

Once, a long time ago, when my Uncle Jack passed away, my relatives including my dad were the pallbearers. My father, who likes a good joke, decided that halfway up the aisle he would knock on the coffin. Uncle Ronnie and Uncle Billy nearly dropped poor Uncle Jack. All I can say is Dad was in the bad books as half the church heard it as well, and Uncle Jack's wife Aunty Daisy fainted, need I say anymore.

No wonder I'm slightly deranged.

CHAPTER 29

It's Christmas – let the madness begin!

I know I say this every year, I hate Christmas, but in truth I adore it. I love the Christmas cards, the decorations, the getting together of family and friends, and of course, I love my grandchildren when they talk about Santa.

How can anyone not like a child's face, so innocent when they tell you what they have put in their letter to Santa?

Parents, please remember that this is the only time of the year when you can bribe your children to behave because Santa is watching, I love it.

In past years when both sets of parents were alive, we would all get together around the dining table and enjoy our meal. Laughter would be the main noise. There were no cell phones at the table only a camera. Just all of us enjoying the day. Then after a huge lunch, we would play the family annual cricket match. Rules did not apply, there weren't any. Although it had lots of drinking and again more laughter. Then somehow, everyone would take time out for an afternoon sleep, and it would begin all over again with dinner.

It's the best time of the year, Merry Christmas everyone!

CHAPTER 30

My Christmas present – my husband is a dickhead!

I can't understand that after 30 years of marriage he still can't go out and buy me a present. I leave clues everywhere. All he has to do is go to the bathroom, there is my perfume, my body lotions, perfumed candles – it's not rocket science. Still, he can't get me anything, and that drives me mad.

I have to buy everyone's presents. Send out the Christmas cards. Do the Christmas shopping for groceries, organize the menu, get the tree, decorate it, decorate the house, and he can't buy one bloody present. He acts like his world has ended, it such a big job for him. Oh, cry me a damn river.

I usually end up getting some clothes that I don't really need. I just pray that one day, he will do something on his own and buy me something, anything. I don't care if it's ugly. The point is it's the thought. Let's face facts, I'm not the only women in the world to have this problem, but you men are such eggheads. Women are so easy to get a gift for. If all else fails then get a voucher for a facial, that would work for me.

So, women of the world, I'm throwing in the towel, he can do all the organizing for Christmas. I'm going on strike and taking time out.

Oh shit! That sounded so good on paper, but it won't happen. I like Christmas to be perfect. Still, I can dream that perhaps one day soon he will surprise me.

No, stop that thought. I don't believe it will be in my lifetime, *ever.*

CHAPTER 31

Surprise, surprise – bet you did not see this coming!

I am the woman who does deserve a husband like mine. I know what all of you are thinking. Especially after my previous chapter about Christmas presents. Well, shut up and listen to this. I will paint you a picture. Christmas day, everyone exchanging gifts, husband looking strange and had been all morning. Chaos was in the room. Wrapping paper everywhere. The room looked like a bomb had hit.

When the man stood up, clinked his glass and asked for attention, the room was quiet. Husband looked at me and invited me to go and stand beside the tree. Where I did find a little square box addressed to 'The women I love.' He had me right there. Nothing else would have mattered, and inside my heart missed a beat.

There was a pair of diamond earrings.

How in the name of everything did he know that I always wanted a pair?

Now admittedly, you have to squint to see the diamonds, but at the end of the day, he got me something.

I must be mad, but I do love this old bloke.

Forget everything I said about him.

CHAPTER 32

Who am I?

Well, that's a hard thing to answer.

So far I am middle aged, I have wobbly bits, I am ready for the knackers yard, my husband still wants to shag me, my kids in their own way need me, and my girlfriends love me. My cats purr at me.

I stare, yet again, at my reflection in the bedroom mirror. This time I am not in my PJ's. I am dressed for dinner, it's my wedding anniversary. I have makeup on, my hair has been styled and colored. I

I'm 50 and Not Out

feel great, I look great, move over Elle McPherson this supermodel is taking over.

Who am I?

I am 50 and fabulous.

Absolutely fabulous.

Bloody fabulous.

And guess what?
I'm not out – well, not yet!
And by the way, I am still a size 14.

THE
END

CONNECT WITH ME ONLINE

Thank you for reading.

Check these links for more from Author Nancy George.

GOODREADS

Add my books to your TBR list on my
Goodreads profile.
https://www.goodreads.com/goodreadscomnancygeorge

AMAZON

Add my books to your TBR list on my
Amazon profile.
https://www.amazon.com/Nancy-
George/e/B01BKW7H7A/ref=dp_byline_cont_ebooks_1

FACEBOOK

https://www.facebook.com/missnancy148/

EMAIL

debfrank@xtra.co.nz

ABOUT THE AUTHOR

Nancy George lives in Wanganui, New Zealand,
with her three cats and her dog Rosie.
Apart from writing, Nancy is a volunteer for the
SPCA fostering kittens.
This is her third book. Her first one is a short story
called "The Silent Scream" and her second is "Girl
in the Shadows"

Printed in Great Britain
by Amazon

86185149R00059